KU-678-613

Blair Makes a Splash

Theresa Breslin

Illustrated by Ken Cox

mammoth

To the real Blair, from Granny B
T.B.

To Margot and Sam
K.C.

ROTHERHAM LIBRARY &
INFORMATION SERVICES

JF

855 982 X

R00024846

SCHOOLS STOCK

First published in Great Britain in 1999
by Mammoth, an imprint of Egmont Children's Books Limited
239 Kensington High Street, London, W8 6SA

Text copyright © 1999 Theresa Breslin
Illustrations copyright © 1999 Ken Cox

The moral rights of the author and illustrator have been asserted

The rights of Theresa Breslin and Ken Cox to be identified as
the author and illustrator of this work have been asserted by them
in accordance with the Copyright, Designs and Patents Act 1988

ISBN 0 7497 3641 0

10 9 8 7 6 5 4 3 2 1

A CIP catalogue record for this book
is available from the British Library

Printed in Great Britain by Cox & Wyman Ltd,
Reading, Berkshire

This paperback is sold subject to the condition that it
shall not, by way of trade or otherwise, be lent, resold,
hired out, or otherwise circulated without the publisher's
prior consent in any form of binding or cover other than
that in which it is published and without a similar
condition including this condition being imposed on
the subsequent purchaser.

Contents

~

1 Blair makes a splash

'I do love to be beside the seaside! Oh, I do love to be beside the sea!' Blair's dad sang in a loud tuneless voice as he pushed Baby Willis in his buggy along the beach, with Gran, Mum, Melissa and Blair following behind.

'Mum, tell Dad to be quiet,' said Blair's big sister, Melissa.

'Tell him yourself,' said Blair's mum.

1

'Being in this family is *so* embarrassing,' said Melissa. She walked faster and caught up with Dad. 'Do you *have* to sing so loudly?' she asked him. 'People are looking at us.'

Dad slowed down. He looked at Melissa in surprise. 'You used to love going to the beach for the day,' he said. 'And you always wanted me to sing that song.'

'That was when I was a *child*,' said Melissa. 'It's different now. It sounds silly.'

Blair's dad stopped at a clear stretch of sand and put the brake on the buggy.

'Actually, Melissa,' he said, 'it sounds exactly the same as it did before. It's you that's different now.' He leaned over the push-chair. 'You like my singing, don't you, Willis?'

'Glug,' said Willis.

'I like it too, Dad,' said Blair, dropping his bucket and spade down on the sand.

2

Blair's dad smiled. 'That's my boy.' He stuck his tongue out at Melissa.

'Oh, for goodness sake!' said Melissa. She flounced away a few metres and spread her towel beside a large rock.

'What's up with Melissa?' asked Blair's gran. She unfolded her deck-chair, put on her sun hat, and sat down carefully.

'My singing seems to upset her,' said Dad.

'Really?' said Gran, and then added under her breath, 'I can't imagine why.' She opened her newspaper and rustled it loudly before settling down to read.

Blair grabbed his inflatable dinosaur from the beach-bag and began to blow it up. 'Can we go swimming, Dad?' he asked.

'Give us a minute or two to get unpacked,' said his dad. He took the beach-umbrella from the pram-tray and stuck it in the sand beside the buggy and then spread towels all around it.

Blair's mum covered Blair, Willis, and herself with lots of sun cream. Then she lay down and closed her eyes.

'Can we go swimming now, Dad?' said Blair.

'Hang on a sec, I'm not even changed yet.'

'Blair, why don't you make Willis a sand castle?' suggested Granny.

Blair picked up his spade and began shovelling furiously.

4

'Oi!' Mum sat up quickly. 'You're throwing sand in my hair! Move away a little bit please, Blair.'

Blair moved along the sand. He began to dig a hole.

'Oi!' Melissa screeched. 'Stop chucking sand about, you horrible monster!'

Blair put his spade down. He looked at his dad. 'Dad, can I go swimming now?' he asked.

'Andy,' said Blair's mum, 'you *did* promise Blair yesterday that you would go swimming with him today.'

Dad groaned. He put down the book

5

that he had just picked up. 'OK, OK,' he said, and began to rummage in the beach-bag for his swimming-shorts.

'Before you go any further,' said Granny, 'I'd like to suggest that you put the car keys away somewhere safe.' She looked over the top of her newspaper. 'It's just that I'd prefer not to have to stay until after midnight looking for them by torchlight, like we did last time we came to the beach.'

'Of course. Of course,' said Dad. He held up the keys for everyone to see. 'Look,' he said, 'I'll put them in the top pocket of my shirt. Now we all know where they are.'

'Dad?' said Blair. 'Can we go swimm –'

'All *right*, Blair,' said Dad.

Blair raced ahead down to the shore. He loved swimming in the sea. Not that he really swam exactly, more splashed about and made running dives.

First he pretended he was a dolphin leaping up and down. Next he was a killer shark lurking beneath the water. Then he was a huge octopus curling long tentacles round its prey.

'This is great, isn't it Dad?' said Blair.

'Fabulous. Em, son . . . do you think you could unwrap your arms and legs from around me? It's making it quite difficult for me to stay afloat'

Mum brought Baby Willis down to play beside the waves. Then Gran came for a paddle, holding up the hem of her flowery dress. Even Melissa came over from her rock for ten minutes and got her swimming costume wet.

After a while, Blair's dad said, 'Aren't you a bit tired now, Blair?'

'No,' said Blair happily. He was being a submarine chugging along trying to spot blue whales through his periscope.

'Blair, why don't you get your fishing-net from the pram-tray and we'll go exploring in the rock pools?' said Gran.

'Do you think we'll find whales in the rock pools?' Blair asked as he went with her.

'More likely seaweed, shells and little crabs.' Granny looked down at Blair. 'Or maybe a mermaid ...'

They didn't find a mermaid but they did find lots of winkles and mussels and tiny shells which Gran said mermaids used to make necklaces. Which probably meant that there were mermaids about, Gran told him.

When the tide came in they packed up and went for a walk along the sea-wall. Dad stopped a passing ice-cream van and bought everyone a cone.

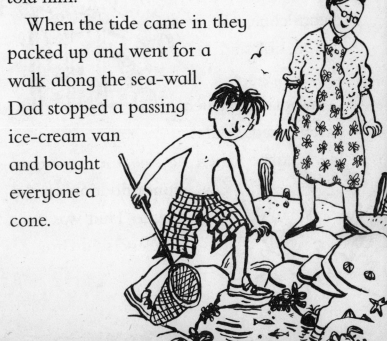

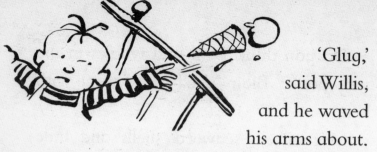

'Glug,'
said Willis,
and he waved
his arms about.

His ice-cream flew out of his hand, through the rail and into the sea.

Splash! went Willis's ice-cream cone.

'Oh, no!' cried Granny and she tried to catch it as it fell.

Splash! went Granny's ice-cream cone.

'Oh, no!' said Blair.

'What's happened here?' asked Dad.

He laughed when he saw the ice-cream cones floating on the water. 'That was a bit careless.'

He leaned
right over
the edge to
get a better
look.

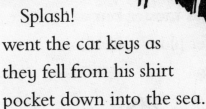

Splash!
went the car keys as
they fell from his shirt
pocket down into the sea.

'Oh, no!' said Dad.

Blair, Dad, Mum, Melissa, Gran and
Willis stared at the water.

'That was a bit careless, Dad,' said Blair.

Blair's dad opened his mouth, then he
closed it again.

'We'll have to find a phone and call the
garage,' said Mum.

'Or Mr Higgins at our D–I–Y shop,' said
Blair. 'He's good at fixing things.'

'Well, he's had plenty of practice in our
house,' said Melissa.

Gran sighed. 'Another midnight journey home from the beach,' she said.

'Dad,' said Blair. 'I've got an idea.'

'Not now, Blair,' said his dad. 'I suppose I could walk to the nearest police station. They might have a master key.'

'I've got a better plan,' said Blair.

'Phone the call-out services?' said Mum.

'No,' said Blair. 'We could –'

'Shhh, Blair,' said his dad. 'I'm trying to think what to do.'

'But, I know what to do!' shouted Blair.

Everybody stared at him. 'What?' they all asked at once.

'This!' said Blair. He knelt down and pulled his fishing-net from the pram-tray. 'We could pull off all the netting, bend the wire to make a hook, and then try to catch the key-ring with it.'

Blair's mum looked at his dad. 'Do you think that might work?' she asked.

'I've always said he was a clever boy,' said Gran proudly as they drove home twenty minutes later. She leaned forward and tapped Blair's dad on the shoulder. 'Be sure to stop at Mr Higgins's shop on the way back,' she said. 'I want to buy Blair a brand new fishing-net. You never know, we might need it again sometime.'

2 Blair visits the dentist

'Aaaarghhh!'

Blair jumped back from his little brother's high chair clutching his finger.

'He bit me!' Blair shouted. 'Willis bit me!'

'Again?' said Blair's dad glancing up from the morning newspaper.

Blair's mum tutted loudly. 'Andy, perhaps

you should explain
to Blair that Willis
doesn't really
know what
he's doing.'

Dad sighed,
folded the news-
paper slowly, and put
it down. He took Blair over to the kitchen
sink and dunked the sore finger in some
cold water. 'Blair,' he said, 'when you put
your finger near Baby Willis's mouth, he
thinks it's food so he snaps with his teeth.'

Blair glared at his little brother. Willis
smiled back. 'Glug,' he said.

A long dribble escaped
from Willis's mouth and
ran down his chin. Mum
wiped it with a tissue.
'Willis is cutting
teeth,' she said. 'He

15

needs something to bite on to help them come through.' She patted Blair on the head. 'It's not that he wants to hurt you.'

Blair examined his finger carefully. 'He could have chopped my finger in half,' he complained. 'It's probably broken.'

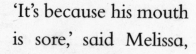

'It's because his mouth is sore,' said Melissa, Blair's big sister. 'You did exactly the same thing to me when you were that age.'

Blair brightened up a little. The thought that he had bitten his big sister at some time, even if he couldn't remember it now, cheered him up.

'I've got a loose tooth at the front,' he said, 'but I don't go around biting people.'

'No,' said Melissa, 'and don't even *think* about trying it, either.'

'Hasn't Ms Dunn, the dentist, something she can give him?' said Blair.

'You know, you're quite right, Blair,' said Mum. 'We are due a family dental check-up.' She smiled at Blair's dad. 'Andy, will you make an appointment, please?'

'OK,' said Blair's dad. He winked at Blair. 'I'll make one for all the men in the family to go together.'

Blair liked going to the dentist. In the waiting-room there were coloured plastic seats in the shape of molars, which were just the right size for him to sit on. There were also lots of picture books to read and toys to play with. And, in her surgery, Ms Dunn always had good drawings and paintings on the walls.

Ms Dunn came in as Blair was looking at one of her new posters. It was a rap poem. 'I'll say it for you while I'm looking at your teeth,' she said. She tapped her little silver mirror on the side of the basin. 'I'll just get the beat. It begins like this . . .

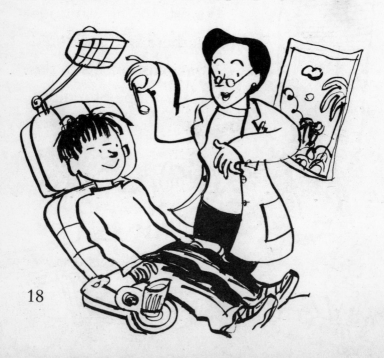

Hey, Guys!
Let's Destroy Deadly
Dee-Kay!
With the dentist's
Hygiene-Routine Rap!

You gotta brush
your teeth
An' I'll tell you why
'Cos when you do
Bacteria die!

You gotta brush your teeth
You gotta clean your
gums
You gotta blast those
germs
They ain't your
chums!

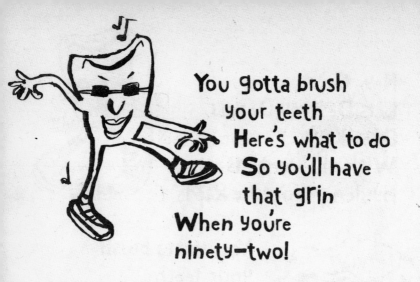

You gotta brush
your teeth
Here's what to do
So you'll have
that grin
When you're
ninety-two!

You gotta brush
your teeth
An' I'll show you how:
Squirt some paste
Grab a toothbrush now!

You gotta brush your teeth
Don't build up plaque
First the front
And then the back

You gotta brush
your teeth
Both up and down
Across the middle
Then round and
round

You gotta brush your teeth
You gotta listen to me
Make sure your drinks
Are sugar free!

You gotta brush
your teeth
Now you know
the way
Fight that monster
Called Dee—Kay!

You gotta brush your
teeth
Give those germs a
ZAP!
With the Hygiene-
Routine
Rap! Rap! Rap!

So . . .
This is how it's
done
First, use your
brush
Then, floss
Then, flush
Spit in the sink

Take a drink
Rinse with
the pink
Mouthwash
Now . . . Big
Smile . . .
WOW!'

'Right on!' said Blair's dad when Ms Dunn had finished. 'I dig that hip rap. Give us five!'

'Pardon?' said Ms Dunn.

'Street poetry, sister,' said Blair's dad. 'I love it. Cool.' He held up his hand, palm flat out. 'Give us five . . . fingers,' he added.

'Oh, I see,' said Ms Dunn. 'Actually, Mr Matthews, in this dental surgery, we say, "Here's lookin' at you . . . Give us thirty-two!"'

Blair's dad looked puzzled. 'Thirty-two?' he said.

'Teeth,' Ms Dunn explained. 'If you add them all up, the molars, the eye-teeth, incisors and wisdom teeth, it comes to thirty-two.'

'Oh . . . right,' said Blair's dad.

'You can jump down now, Blair,' said Ms Dunn. 'You have terrific teeth. There's one loose at the front but it will come out by itself.'

While Blair's dad was having his teeth scaled and polished, Blair did the actions of the Hygiene-Routine Rap, and wobbled his loose front tooth backwards and forwards with his finger. Just as Ms Dunn finished, it came away in his hand. 'Look.' He showed her the tooth.

'That's a cracker,' said Ms Dunn. 'Worth at least fifty pence from the tooth fairy.'

Blair glanced at his dad. 'I heard,' he said in a loud voice, 'that some tooth fairies leave two pound coins.'

'Not in our house they don't,' said his dad.

He lifted Willis on to his knee and Ms Dunn peered into the baby's mouth.

'This little fellow has no problems at all,' she said. 'Just make sure he has some hard rusks to chew on to help those first teeth come through.'

She laughed. 'And don't put your fingers too close to his mouth. Babies can bite quite hard.'

'Oh, we know that,' said Dad. He put Baby Willis into his push-chair. 'He won't catch me out, that's for sure.'

Ms Dunn gave Blair a clean tissue to wrap round his tooth. Then she rolled up a copy of her Hygiene-Routine Rap poster and handed it to him.

'You might want to put this up on your bedroom wall,' she said. 'See you all in six months.'

'Thank you,' said Blair.

'Glug,' said Willis, and a dribble spilled out of his mouth.

'Bye,' said Blair's dad as he leaned over the top of the push-chair to mop it up.

Suddenly he leaped back.

'Aaaarghhh!' he shouted. 'He bit me! Willis bit me!'

3 Blair's fishing trip

'Are you absolutely sure you've got everything you need, dear?' said Blair's mum.

'Just about.'

Blair's dad pulled firmly on the last strap of the roof rack. On top of the car were piled Baby Willis's changing mat, two folding canvas chairs, an umbrella, a windbreak, two fishing-rods with rod-rests, and a waterproof bundle containing a groundsheet, a blanket, and a travelling-rug.

'That should do it now,' said Blair's dad as he tightened the buckle. Then he went round to close the boot.

Crammed inside the boot were a picnic hamper, wellingtons, jumpers, raincoats, scarves, woolly hats, a folded push-chair, a holdall with nappies, baby food and bottle, Dad's rucksack, Blair's rucksack, and the fishing-bag with bait, reels and weights.

'No room for anything else anyway,' muttered Blair's gran. She moved to the side of the driveway to chat to their next door neighbours.

'He's been loading that car for the past three hours,' said old Mr Fletcher loudly. 'There's everything in there bar the kitchen sink.'

'*Sshhh*, Dad!' said Mavis, Mr Fletcher's daughter. 'Mr Matthews going somewhere nice?' she asked Blair's gran.

'He's taking Blair and Willis on a fishing trip,' said Gran.

'How long will they be away for, then?' Mavis asked.

'Just for the day.'

'Good grief!' said old Mr Fletcher.

'Sshhh, *Dad*!' said Mr Fletcher's daughter Mavis.

Blair's dad strapped Willis securely in his baby-seat. Then Blair climbed in beside his little brother and put his own safety belt on.

'We're off then,' said Dad.

'About time too,' said old Mr Fletcher.

'*Sshhh! Dad*!' said Mavis.

30

Blair's dad drove for about an hour until he found a good spot beside a river just beyond a big retail park. There they spread out the ground-sheet and travelling-rug, and unpacked the picnic hamper. Dad set up the windbreak and put Baby Willis in his push-chair. They put their fishing-rods up on the rod-rests. Then they unfolded their canvas

31

chairs and sat down.

'This is the life, eh, son?' said Dad a few hours later.

'Actually,' said Blair, 'it's a bit boring.' He waggled his fishing-rod up and down on its rest. 'I mean, I didn't know that nothing actually *happens* when you're fishing.'

'That's the great thing about it,' said Blair's dad. He munched happily on his cheese roll. 'Getting close to nature . . . the outdoor life . . . living in the wild.'

'But we're not,' said Blair. 'We've been here for *ages* and look at all we've caught.'

Lying on the riverbank beside them

were some rusty cans, a black bin bag, and an awful lot of pondweed.

'It's the taking part that counts,' said Dad. 'I'm having a great time.'

'Ummm . . .' said Blair doubtfully. 'I'd really like to catch *something*, Dad. I told Mum we'd bring her back some fish to cook for dinner tonight.'

'Well let's have one last go,' said Dad. 'Bring me the bait tin. It's beside the push-chair.'

'We're almost out of bait,' said Blair holding the tin for Dad to see.

'That's impossible. There were dozens of maggots in there.' Blair's dad looked in the empty tin. Then he looked at Baby Willis. Then he looked in the empty tin again.

'Glug,' said Baby Willis.

'Oh no!' said Dad. 'No wonder he wouldn't eat his baby food.' He hastily swallowed the rest of his cheese roll. 'I think we'll pack up and go home now, Blair.'

'It's not fair,' said Blair. 'I especially wanted to be a fisherman today!'

Blair's dad began loading the car and Blair went to gather up the fishing-rods. Just as he lifted his, he felt the most tremendous tug! 'I've caught something, Dad!' he shrieked. 'I've caught something!'

His dad ran to help. 'It's a huge one!' he shouted. 'A twenty pounder at least!'

The rod bent under the weight. They reeled in with all their might.

'I'll have to wade in,' said Dad. 'Good job I brought my wellies.'

Blair's dad splashed into the water. Blair held on to his rod as hard as he could. What could be caught on the end of his line? Perhaps it was a gi-normous conger eel, or a mammoth man-eating manatee? Blair was sure he could see its huge tail thrashing about in the water.

'Err . . . Blair,' said Dad after a moment or two.

Blair looked up. His dad had pulled the end of a supermarket trolley out of the water.

35

'Sorry, son, your line must have snagged in the wire mesh as you lifted your rod.'

Blair flung down his rod. He glared at the supermarket trolley. Then he looked at it again. He was remembering something his gran had told him.

'Listen, Dad, did you know that at the supermarket they pay a reward for returned trolleys?'

'No I didn't know that,' said Blair's dad. He looked at Blair. 'Blair,' he said, 'did you know that they also sell fish in the supermarket?'

'That's amazing!' said Blair's mum as she unwrapped the parcel which Blair's dad gave her. 'Four rainbow trout, and all of them almost exactly the same size! I didn't realise that you two were such good fishermen!'

'Part of it is knowing where to go to get the best catch,' said Blair's dad. He winked at Blair.

'Yes,' said Blair. He put down his rucksack and opened it. 'And I even remembered that Willis and Gran don't like fish bones. So, when you were strapping Willis into the car in the car park, Dad, I ran back and caught something else for them.'

Blair pulled a damp package from inside his rucksack. He smiled happily at his dad, and then he handed his mum a packet of frozen fish fingers.

4 Blair's tree-house

From the landing Blair could see his big
sister putting up posters in her bedroom.

'Can I borrow the hammer when you're
finished?' he asked.

'You must be joking!' said Melissa. She
stopped what she was doing for a moment
to look at her young brother. 'There is *no
way* that anyone in their right mind is

going to let *you* anywhere near a hammer, what with your reputation as a demolition expert. And another thing,' she marched across her bedroom floor, 'do remember that my room is *strictly* off-limits to grotty little boys.' She slammed the door with a crash.

'Didn't want to go in your stupid room anyway,' Blair said in a loud voice. 'Your room is . . . is . . . *boring*.'

Which wasn't actually true. Blair found Melissa's room extremely interesting. On her desk she kept stacks of bottles, pots, jars

and canisters which were full of things which were really useful for Blair's games. Sometimes he went on secret raiding missions. Multi-coloured nail varnish, sticky face-glitter and purple hair-mousse were just some of the items which he had 'borrowed' from his sister's room from time to time.

Blair made a rude face at Melissa's door and then trailed downstairs to the living-room where his mum and dad sat talking.

'Melissa won't lend me the hammer,' he said.

'So your sister *has* a brain,' murmured Blair's dad.

'Thank goodness for that,' said Blair's mum.

'Melissa's being mean,' said Blair. 'She's almost finished using it.'

'That's not the point, Blair,' Mum said. 'You wouldn't be allowed the hammer even if no one was using it.'

'Why not?' asked Blair.

Blair's mum and dad looked at each other.

'Umm . . . Could you explain that to him, dear,' said Mum.

'Because quite enough of the family budget is spent in Mr and Mrs Higgins's D-I-Y shop already,' said Dad under his breath.

'Look, son,' he said out loud, 'do you remember last month when you borrowed the screwdriver?'

'I was only trying to help out,' Blair protested. 'You kept saying that the screws on the garage door needed sorting.'

'I know I did,' said Dad. 'But by

41

"sorting" I meant tightened up, not loosened so that the garage door fell off just as I was parking the car.'

'I said I was sorry,' said Blair. 'And Mr Higgins told me that the car bonnet already had a dent in it, and that we probably needed a new car anyway.'

'Did he?' said Dad. 'Well, there was also the time you picked up the garden shears when I put them down for a minute.'

'That was rather careless of you though, Andy,' said Mum. 'You shouldn't leave dangerous tools lying about.'

'Anyhow, Granny's leg is nearly better now,' said Blair.

'You can't have the

hammer, Blair,' his dad said firmly.

Blair folded his arms across his chest. 'It's always the same,' he said. 'I'm never allowed to do *anything* I want to.'

Blair's gran came into the living-room carrying Baby Willis.

'This little laddie's all bathed and changed,' she said.

She handed Willis over to Blair's dad, and then she noticed the expression on Blair's face. 'And what's the matter with you tonight, young man?'

43

'He wants to borrow the hammer,' said Blair's mum.

'Oh,' said Gran.

'Exactly,' said Mum.

'What do you need a hammer for, Blair?' Gran asked him.

'I want to build a tree-house.'

'A tree-house!' said Mum.

Gran thought carefully for a bit. 'You don't need a hammer to build a tree-house,' she said at last.

'If we let him build a tree-house,' said Mum, 'he is more than likely to fall out of it and break his neck.'

'Mmm . . .' said Gran. 'That might depend on where exactly you build it.' She looked out of the window. 'It's a lovely evening,' she said. 'A few hours of daylight left.' She held out her hand. 'Come on, Blair, let's see if your old granny can remember anything she learned in the Girl Guides.'

First of all they drove to Mr and Mrs Higgins's D-I-Y shop to get some supplies.

'We're not keeping you from closing up?' asked Gran.

'Not at all,' said Mrs Higgins. 'Nothing is too much trouble for our best customers.'

When Granny explained what they wanted to do, Mr and Mrs Higgins began searching in the back store for anything that might be useful. They brought out some odd pieces of slotted small wooden fencing, lots of twine, a piece of polysheeting, and some other odds and ends. Then Blair and his gran got some good tips from Mr and Mrs Higgins on the best way to fit the wooden fencing together, and how to place the sheeting across the top.

In Blair's back garden, Granny found the best place to build. Blair and his gran slotted the fence pieces

together and tied
the polysheeting
across the
top. Along
one wall

Blair screwed in six big cup-hooks to hang things on. Then Gran showed him how to make bookshelves with brick supports at each end.

Blair ran back up the path to fetch his comics and books. 'I'm building a tree-house,' he told their next door neighbours.

Old Mr Fletcher peered up into the trees at the foot of Blair's garden. 'There's nothing there,' he said.

'*Shhh*, Dad,' said his
daughter, Mavis.

Mavis went into their house and came out again a moment later. She handed some old cushions over the hedge to Blair. 'That will do if you have visitors,' she said.

'You'll need to give them a map and a compass to find it,' muttered her dad.

'*Shhh, Dad*!' said Mavis.

Blair put his comics and books on the shelves and his Fighting Fantasy Figures along the top. Gran stuck up a few pictures. When they were finished, Blair pinned a notice on the door.

Blair went into the kitchen. 'Gran and I need juice and biscuits,' he told his mum.

Blair's Tree-House
PRIVATE
Keep Out
That means YOU

'We'll be having our opening party soon. A tree-house-warming.'

Blair's dad looked out of the window at the trees. 'I can't see anything,' he said.

'It's not *there*,' said Blair.

Melissa laughed. 'If it's an invisible tree-house,' she said, 'how can we come to your party?'

'You might not get invited,' said Blair. He lifted the tray with his juice and biscuits and marched out the door.

Gran had found an old crate in the garage to use as a table. Blair put the tray down on it.

'Mr Fletcher says people will need a map to find us,' said Blair.

'We'll draw one on the back of our

invitations, then,' said Granny.

They wrote them out carefully in felt-tip pen. Then Blair delivered them.

'Well, what do think?' Gran asked everybody as she offered them biscuits and juice. 'Do you like Blair's tree-house?'

'As it's as far away from the house as is possible, it's got my vote,' said Melissa.

'Indeed,' said Blair's dad looking around, 'it is in a very interesting position for a tree-house.'

'Not too windy,' said old Mr Fletcher. 'You build a tree-house too high,' he told Blair, 'come the winter it just blows away.' He dipped his biscuit in his juice to soften it and then sucked the end.

'Really, Dad!' said Mavis.

'Glug,' said Baby Willis.

'I think it's wonderful,' said Blair's mum. 'There is nothing cracked, smashed or broken, and no one is in the hospital Casualty Department. Underneath the rhododendron bushes seems to me to be an excellent place to build a tree-house.'

'Yes,' said Blair happily. 'Granny was right. A tree-house doesn't really *need* to be up a tree.'

If you enjoyed this
MAMMOTH STORYBOOK
look out for:

Blair the Winner

Theresa Breslin
Illustrated by *Ken Cox*

~

It's not fair being in the middle,
like Blair.

Little Baby Willis is a pest.
Big sister, Melissa,
thinks Blair's the pest.

And all the family never stop nagging!

But it's Blair who saves the day on a
camping trip that goes wrong . . .

If you enjoyed this
MAMMOTH STORYBOOK
look out for:

Allie's Rabbit

Helen Dunmore
Illustrated by *Simone Lia*

~

Allie has wanted a rabbit for ages
and ages.
She's saved enough money and she's
chosen the rabbit she likes best in the
pet shop.

But Mum still says no!

Now Allie has a plan . . .

Can she persuade her big sister
Jacqueline to help her?

If you enjoyed this
MAMMOTH STORYBOOK
look out for:

Only Molly

Cally Poplak
Illustrated by *Alison Bartlett*

~

Molly is special . . .

One day Molly and her mum come
back from school and find an unwanted
visitor . . .

One day Molly goes out with her Aunt
Jan and something embarrassing happens
– but something wonderful too . . .

One day Molly and Mum go fishing with
Tim and Rosy and see something scary . . .

And then Molly is invited to a party . . .
and gets the loveliest surprise of
all!

If you enjoyed this
MAMMOTH STORYBOOK
look out for:

Thief in the Garden

Elizabeth Arnold
Illustrated by *Ailie Busby*

~

Mum is so busy looking after Grandad
that she doesn't have much time for
Josh and Connor.

But there is one brilliant thing about
living with Grandad –
his fantastic wild garden.

Especially when the boys find a stray
cat there.

How can they persuade Mum to
let them keep him?

If you enjoyed this

MAMMOTH STORYBOOK

look out for:

No More Pets!

Cally Poplak
Illustrated by *Alison Bartlett*

~

Beth's mother has a rule: 'No Pets!' The
flat's just too small.

So when a friend gives Beth a goldfish as a
present, what will Mum say?

And when a cuddly cat and a bouncing
dog appear on the scene too, how can Beth
turn them away?

An animal-filled story for anyone who
has ever wanted a
pet.

If you enjoyed this
MAMMOTH STORYBOOK
look out for:

Pest Friends

Pippa Goodhart
Illustrated by *Louise Armour-Chelu*

~

Maxine is big and loud and funny.

Minnie is small and quiet and shy.

They are the best of friends – but don't
ask why!

At school and at home, they are never
apart.

Then Minnie loses a tooth – and she's in
danger of losing her best friend too . . .

If you enjoyed this
MAMMOTH STORYBOOK
look out for:

Tyler and the Talk Stalk

Annie Dalton
Illustrated by *Brett Hudson*

~

Tyler doesn't see the point of those boring
school bean experiments, until he's given
three special beans.
Now Tyler can bring back the magic to
Darkwoods Estate.

Thanks to Tyler, his class goes on a
fantastic adventure to the land of giants,
where he finds out who's behind the latest
daring robberies.